GLORIA'S LENS

AUTHOR: LAUREN JONES
ILLUSTRATOR: LAUREN HAINES &
LAUREN JONES

JOHA
creations & publishing company

www.gloriaslens.com

published by JOHA creations & publishing
www.johacreations.com

printed in China

Up high on a rock in a place
not too far from here,
sat a perfect tiny town.
Or so from a distance
it would appear.

Every mouth had on a smile. Teeth were polished and white.
Everything at first glance seemed just about right.
The streets, the yards, the homes were all tidy.
The streetlamps, the cars, even the doorknobs were shiny!

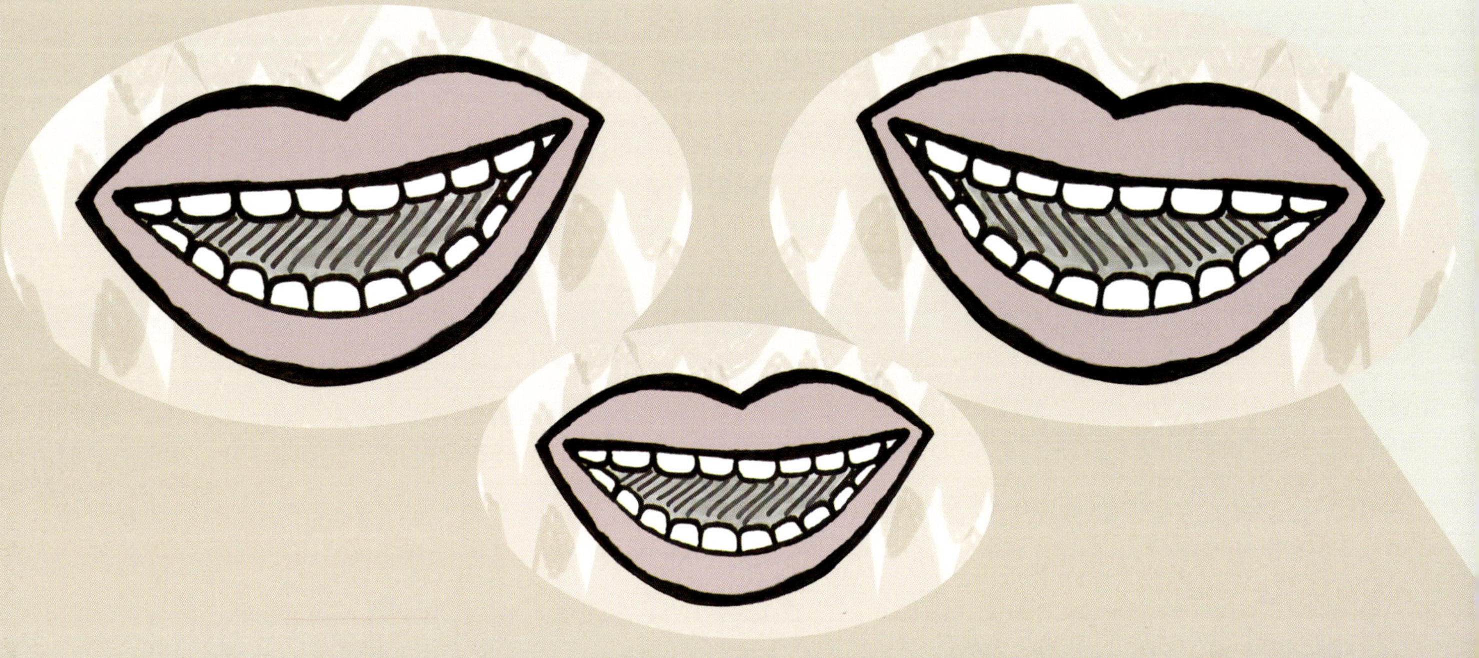

Shirts were tucked in with a belt and a tie,
purple skirts for the girls, and green pants for the guys.

See choices were few;
there was no time to choose.
The Authority set rules
that told all what to do.

RULES

1. SMILE AT ALL TIMES.
2. BE PERFECTLY TIDY AND NEAT.
3. BE LED BY THE CLOCK.

All was set in place; the townspeople didn't have to think.
If you were thirsty, you would have Blue or Pink Drink.
No one had met the Authority or even seen his face.

It was the townspeople who enforced the rules without favor or grace.
See when people didn't smile or forgot to shine their shoes,
they were scolded and punished and sent to their rooms.

PEE

All had jars in their pockets they would carry around
for when someone acted strange
or did something not written down.
There were bitter herbs in these jars and everyone knew
they were sour and icky and smelled like...

The worst part was the herbs stained teeth bright green!
It took hours of scrubbing to get them all clean.

One family, in this tiny town set high on a rock,
who obeyed all the rules and was led by the clock,
had a daughter named Gloria who was small and petite.
She tried to always smile, and be tidy and neat.
Gloria obeyed all the rules and never asked why,
But sometimes she had an idea that she just had to try.

One day as she went to fill up her drink
she thought to herself, "What if I mix Blue with Pink?"
She tried it out, not knowing what it would do.
She thought, "This is quite yummy!
I MADE SOMETHING NEW!"

Just then her mother walked in
and saw what she had done.
"Oh NO, Gloria!
You must only choose ONE!"
She reached in her pocket
and yanked out the herbs.
"This will teach you, Gloria...
One day you will learn!"

Gloria opened her mouth
and let out a sigh.
She swallowed the herbs
and she tried not to cry.

She was sent to her room

to start scrubbing her teeth.

She saw her neatly made bed
and wanted to crawl underneath.

Minutes went by and slowly the shame began to fade.
“That was actually a pretty neat drink that I made!”
She smiled to herself and then giggled aloud.
She had made something new! Her heart felt so proud!
She began swinging her arms up and then down,
spinning in circles and dancing around!

"No, NO! Gloria!" Her mother said as she walked in the room.
"This is NOT on the clock! This is NOT what we do!
No dancing allowed in this house or this town!
The Authority will see you! He is watching you now.
Here are more herbs. Stay in your room!
You need to feel shame. Yes, Gloria! Shame on YOU!"

Gloria looked in the mirror,
her teeth now dark green.
How could she ever face the world?
How could she ever be seen?

Just then like lightning, like a thunderous CLAP!
Her room lit up and something fell in her lap.
It was small and round, and clear on both ends.
It was the size of an eye, but looked more like a lens.

She stood up and looked through it
and couldn't believe what she saw!
The colors were brighter and she was now tall!

She ran to the mirror and was surprised at the sight,
her teeth were not green, they were sparkling white!
Then just like lightning she heard a voice in her room,
"This is *my* lens, this is how I see you."
"Who are you?" she cried, "Why are you here?"
"Listen close my loved one, and do not have fear."

"I am the Rock on which this town was built.
I take away all worry, all shame, and all guilt.
Go out on the street and look through my lens.
I want to show you who the *true* Authority is."

Quickly she jumped up and ran out the door
with more excitement than she'd ever felt before!
Right out the door, she looked down at the street.
She saw words through the lens as if written in ink.

"You were created by me to walk on these streets,
to talk, and to laugh, and to dance, and to think!
I loved your fun thought to make that new drink!
Man made these rules but they are not true.
Now go and show them as I have shown you."

She ran down the street and started dancing around,
not caring about green teeth or the eyes of the town.
The townspeople gasped when they saw her
and pulled out their herbs.
But she showed them the lens and all these new words!

They read the words on the street on the rock where they stood.

They were stories of love, friendship, and good!

"Pour out those bitter herbs onto the street.
I have sweet *new* bread for you to eat."
They quickly pulled out their herbs and poured them all out.
They all felt so free that they let out a shout!!!

AAHHOOO!

Their Authority was with them! They could now hear his voice!
He wasn't giving them shame, he was giving them choice!
Their Authority was with them! His love they could feel,
and for the first time in their lives, their smiles were REAL!!!